Believe that

Written by **Kelly MacDonald**

Illustrations by ***Bogdan Luca***

Library and Archives Canada Cataloguing in Publication

MacDonald, Kelly, 1958-
        Believe that you can! / written by Kelly MacDonald ; illustrations by Bogdan Luca.

(Life's lessons ; no. 2)
ISBN 0-9736893-1-5

        I. Luca, Bogdan II. Title. III. Series: MacDonald, Kelly, 1958-
Life's Lessons on ice ; no. 2

PS8625.D64B45 2006   jC813'.6   C2006-900989-9

Layout: Kimberley Young
Printed and bound in Canada

www.lifeslessonsonice.com

What I Learned from Playing Soccer...
"...I have to practice my skills and believe that I can accomplish my goals, in order to reach them."

To Ron & Vicki
...who taught me that I can do anything
if I work hard and believe in myself.

**O**ur team had been losing,

Just losing all season,

We could not figure out

The rhyme or the reason,

We played as a team

We were good — we were bad

That just had to be

The worst season we'd had.

We won the odd few

Maybe one, maybe two

But try as we might,

It was all we could do.

e cried and we practiced
We focused and thought
We were on a rough course
We were in a tough spot.

So we thought what we'd do
We would bring in new plays,
So that's what we did
And we practiced for days.

We played our next game,
And the next and one after,
It was hard to hear over
All the fan's laughter.

We still did not have it
The secret, the treasure
We still were not reaching
Even close to the measure.

We all got new jerseys,
New cleats, a new ball
But it still didn't change us
We'd hit a big wall.

S o we redid our plays
And we fine tuned our lines
We bought a good luck charm
We focused our minds—

But nothing had changed
We still sat at the end
Of the stats in the paper
We could not pretend—

**T**hat nothing was wrong,
But what could it be?
Think as we might
We still could not see

So we played on and on
Through that long losing season
And then brought in a guru
To discover the reason,

That every time

We had the ball

We would play like we should

And still we would fall

To the roundest of numbers,

The zero, the naught,

It seemed not to matter

If we took a shot!

**O**ur guru, he watched

He was quiet, a thinker

He did not a thing,

Not a tweak, not a tinker,

By the end of the game,

He called us together

He did not blame us

Or the grass or the weather,

e told us our thoughts

Were the cause of our losses,

Not our cleats, not our plays,

Not the grass, not our bosses.

Now how could it be

That our thoughts make us lose?

Well our thoughts create magic

If we so choose,

They can create goals

And good play and bad

They can create chaos

They can make us sad.

Thoughts create anger

And famine and war

They can create fights,

And losses and more,

But they can also create

A much better place

They can create laughter

Put a smile on our face.

He said that for us,

In order to win,

We needed to develop

Some talent within,

 et past our mistakes
And soar straight ahead
Play our best each time out
Keep good thoughts in our heads.

We must think we can win
At the end of each play
Our thoughts are our power
Our key to great play.

o win, score or lose it

Our thoughts were the key

If we could just think it

We could make it be!

We've got to believe

As we walk onto the grass

That all that we do

If we score, kick or pass

 o matter the position
No matter the play
Thinking we can
Will push it our way!

The feeling got stronger
With each game we played
Our record got better
With each passing day.

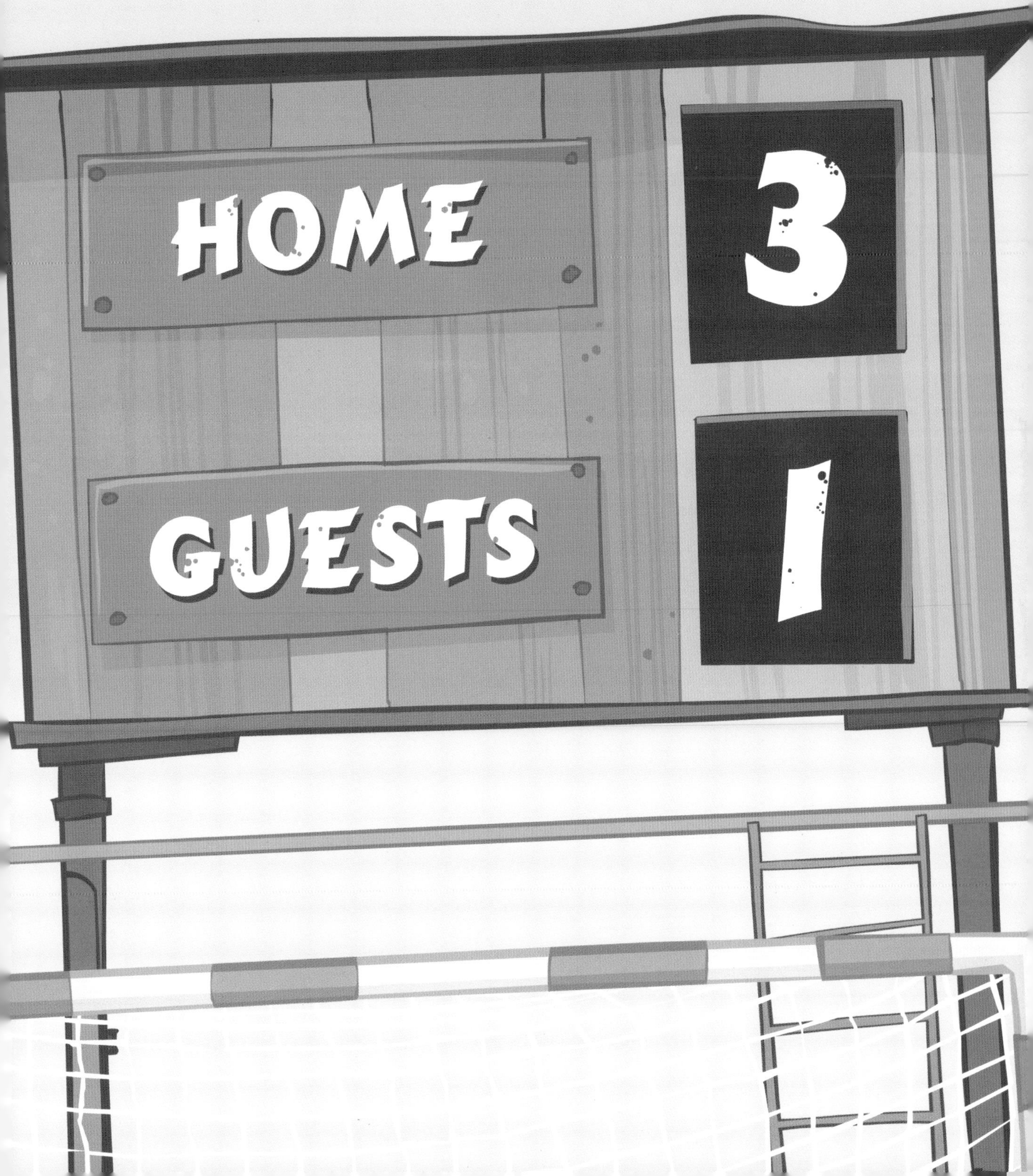
HOME
3
GUESTS
1

 **A**nd winning a game,

And playing it well,

Makes believing it easy

And now you can tell

The crowd is not laughing

The guru was right

We know we can win

With all of our might!

(Tell everyone you know!)

What I Learned from Playing Soccer…

1. I have to practice my skills and believe
that I can accomplish my goals, in order to reach them.

2. Sometimes I win and sometimes I lose!

3. I give my best every time, regardless of the score.

4. Sometimes I am a hero, and other times I am not!

5. Playing for the team will get me further
than playing for personal glory!

6. There will be coaches I like and those that I do not like.
Either I make it work or I move on.

7. I will learn from my mistakes and move on to the next play.

ENJOY THE GAME!